Welcome to
The
Hen-House

First published in 2004 in Great Britain by
Gullane Children's Books.
an imprint of Pinwheel Limited
Winchester House.
259-269 Old Marylebone Road.
London NW1 5XJ

1 2 3 4 5 6 7 8 9 10

Text and illustrations © Jude Wisdom 2004

The right of Jude Wisdom to be identified as
the author and illustrator of this work
has been asserted by her in accordance with
the Copyright. Designs. and Patents Act. 1988.

A CIP record for this title is available from the British Library.

ISBN 1-86233-434-X

Printed and bound in Belgium

To Daisy, who dreamt up the story....

Kate - "The Textile Queen"....

Miss Chicken and the Hungry Neighbour

and Jack.

Jude Wisdom

GULLANE
CHILDREN'S BOOKS

Miss Chicken had never
been out of the hen-house.
"It's high time I found a place
of my own!" she thought.

So she spread her wings,
flew to the edge of town
and landed right next to a little house.
It was pink and it was pretty,
with a neat back garden to grow
whatever she needed for dinner.

Mother Hen rang up to see
how she was settling in.
"What is your neighbour
like, dear?" she clucked.

Miss Chicken peered
out of the window.
"Very large, with a long snout,
two ears and a hungry look
on his face," she said.

Mother Hen squawked in alarm.
"That sounds very much like a wolf
to me!" she cried. "Now listen, my dear,
you must be careful! Wolves are big and bad
and they eat hens like us for breakfast.
Oh, if only you'd stayed in the hen-house!"

Miss Chicken tried not to let Mother Hen's words worry her.
She set to work on her vegetable patch
and soon forgot about the wolf, until . . .

"Good evening, Miss Chicken!"
said a voice. It came from next door.

"So sorry to have
startled you . . ."
began her neighbour.

Of course, as you see, her neighbour wasn't a wolf at all. He was Mr Trotter, a happy pig. But how was Miss Chicken to know? She didn't know about pigs, or wolves, or anything much at all, because she had never been out of the hen-house.

Miss Chicken dropped her spade and ran into the house in a flurry of feathers.

Mr Trotter scratched his snout.

"What an odd bird!" he said to himself. He had been about to invite her round for tea.

"Still," he thought cheerfully, "all the more cake for me!"

Miss Chicken was straight on
the phone to Mother Hen.
"You were right about the wolf,"
she squawked. "He tried to
gobble me up in the
vegetable patch!"

"I knew this
would happen!"
shrieked Mother Hen.
"Doodle, do
be sensible and come
home to the hen-house,
there's a dear!"

But Miss Chicken was determined to stay put. That night she hatched a plan. "I'll build an enormous wall," she decided. "It will keep the wolf out and I can grow my vegetables in peace."

Within the week the wall was up. Mr Trotter was puzzled. "What's she up to now?" he wondered. "I'll take a tiny peek . . ." Mr Trotter scratched and snuffled and scrambled himself a tunnel under the wall . . .

and squeezed his way through it. What a sight for sore eyes!
Miss Chicken's vegetables had sprouted
in the warm summer sun.
Mr Trotter's mouth began to water.
So many juicy vegetables! Perhaps
he could try just one little carrot . . .

But
as well
as being a
happy pig,
Mr Trotter was
also a very greedy pig, and
before you could say,

"Eat up your greens!"

he had *munched*
and *crunched* and
gobbled up every single
vegetable in the patch.

"Oh no!" he groaned,
looking at his bulging tummy.
"How on earth could that have happened?"

He tried to scrabble his way
back through the wall.
But Mr Trotter's tummy
was far too full.

"Help!" he squealed.
"Help, I'm stuck!"

When Miss Chicken looked out of her
window, she could hardly believe her eyes!
In a real flap, she phoned Mother Hen.
"The wolf has eaten all my vegetables and his bottom
is sticking out from under my wall!" she cried.

Trying to hide her alarm, Mother Hen told Miss Chicken
to keep her beak up and wait for the rescue party
that would soon be on its way.

But Miss Chicken
grew tired of waiting.
"I can't stay cooped up in
here all day," she thought.
She peeped out of the
window and there was her
neighbour's round bottom and
curly tail, still sticking out
of the hole.

"He doesn't look fierce!"
she thought. "Perhaps
I should go and
chat to him."

Miss Chicken crept down the garden path.

"Help!" cried Mr Trotter. He didn't sound fierce, either. Miss Chicken decided to pull him out.

So she *heaved* and she *hoed*, she *huffed* and she *puffed*, until finally . . .

POP! ...out of the hole shot Mr Trotter.

His face was red with embarrassment. "I'm so sorry, Miss Chicken!" he gasped. "I didn't mean to eat all your greens - but there's nothing I love more than munching on gorgeous juicy vegetables."

Miss Chicken was confused.

"But," she said, "I thought you were a big bad wolf who eats hens like me for breakfast!"

"Whatever gave you that idea?" chuckled Mr Trotter.

"I'm not a wolf . . . I'm just a happy pig!"

When Mother Hen's rescue party
arrived, Mr Trotter and Miss Chicken
were enjoying a nice cup of tea.
They had become the best of friends.

"I must say, dear . . ." clucked Mother Hen as Mr Trotter passed round
his homemade cakes, "he does seem awfully polite - for a wolf!"
"That's because he isn't a wolf at all!" laughed Miss Chicken.
"He's what you call a pig, Mother Hen!"

"Is that so?" remarked Mother Hen.
"Well, you could knock me down with a feather.
I really must get out of the hen-house more often!"